P9-DCC-645

with a little help from my friends

written by John Lennon and Paul McCartney
illustrated by Henry Cole

LITTLE SIMON
New York London Toronto Sydney New Delhi

LITTLE SIMON
An imprint of Simon & Schuster Children's Publishing Division
1230 Avenue of the Americas, New York, New York 10020
First Little Simon hardcover edition December 2019

For information about special discounts for bulk purchases, please contact Simon & Schuster Special Sales at 1-866-506-1949 or business@simonandschuster.com.

The Simon & Schuster Speakers Bureau can bring authors to your live event. For more information or to book an event contact the Simon & Schuster Speakers Bureau at 1-866-248-3049 or visit our website at www.simonspeakers.com.

Designed by Dan Potash

Manufactured in China 0919 SCP

10 9 8 7 6 5 4 3 2 1

This book has been cataloged with the Library of Congress. ISBN 978-1-5344-2983-3 ISBN 978-1-5344-2984-0 (eBook)

What would you think
if I sang out of tune?

Would you stand up
and walk out on me?

Lend me your ears
and I'll sing you a song,

and I'll try not to sing out of key.

Oh, I get by with a little help from my friends.

Mmm, I get high with a little help from my friends.

Mmm, gonna try with a little help from my friends.

What do I do

when my love is away?

Does it worry you

to be alone?

How do I feel
by the end
of the day?

Are you sad because
you're on your own?

No, I get by with a little
help from my friends.

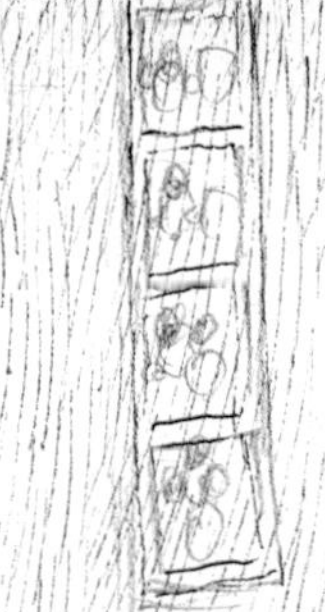

Mmm, I get high with a
little help from my friends.

Mmm, gonna try with a
little help from my friends.

Do you need anybody?

I need somebody to love.

Could it be anybody?

I want somebody to love.

Would you believe
in a love at first sight?

Yes, I'm certain that
it happens all the time.

What do you see
when you turn out the light?

I can't tell you, but
I know it's mine.

Oh, I get by with a little help from my friends.

Mmm, I get high with a little help from my friends.

Oh, I'm gonna try with a
little help from my friends.

Do you need anybody?

I just need someone to love.

Could it be anybody?

I want somebody to love.

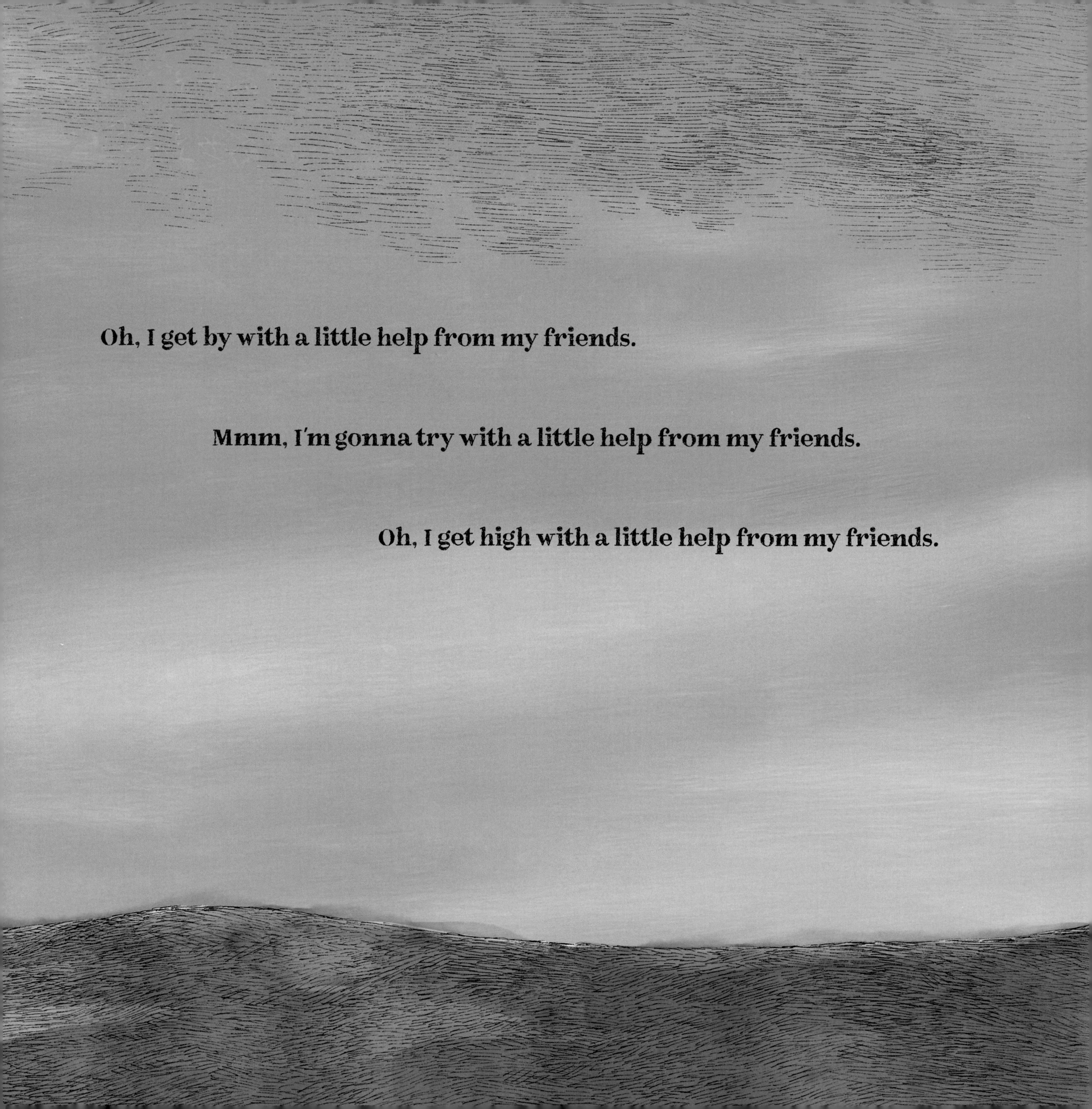

Oh, I get by with a little help from my friends.

Mmm, I'm gonna try with a little help from my friends.

Oh, I get high with a little help from my friends.

Yes, I get by with a little help from my friends . . .

with a little help from my friends!